Topsy and Tim
Go to the Doctor

By Jean and Gareth Adamson

Illustrations by Belinda Worsley

A catalogue record for this book is available from the British Library

Published by Ladybird Books Ltd
A Penguin Company
Penguin Books Ltd., 80 Strand, London WC2R 0RL, UK
Penguin Books Australia Ltd., 707 Collins Street, Melbourne, Victoria 3008, Australia
Penguin Group (NZ) 67 Apollo Drive, Rosedale, North Shore 0632, New Zealand

003

ISBN: 978-1-40930-334-3
Printed in China

www.topsyandtim.com

It was a cold and misty morning. Mummy cooked
a tasty hot breakfast for Topsy and Tim.
"Don't want any breakfast," said Tim.

"Oh, you are a misery," said Mummy crossly. Dad was not cross, but then he had not cooked the breakfast.

"This isn't like Tim," he said.
"There must be something wrong.
Open your mouth wide, Tim."
Tim's throat was swollen and red.
"Poor old Tim," said Dad.

Mummy phoned the Health Centre. She made an appointment for Tim to see Dr Sims. They walked to the Health Centre. Tim wore his scarf up over his nose to keep his sore throat warm.

The receptionist checked Tim's appointment on her computer.
She told them to go and wait outside Dr Sims' surgery.
"Look," said Topsy. "There's Kerry."
Kerry was one of Topsy and Tim's school friends.

"What's the matter, Kerry?" asked Topsy.
"It hurts when I swallow," Kerry said.
"Tim has a sore throat too," said Topsy.
Tim just looked glum.

Soon it was Tim's turn to go into the surgery. "Good morning," said Dr Sims.

"Good morning, Dr Sims," said Topsy.
Tim said nothing.
"Tim isn't talking," Topsy explained.
"I think it's because his throat hurts."

"Open your mouth, Tim," said Dr Sims, "and let me see."
Dr Sims took a little flat stick and held it on Tim's tongue.
"Say ah," he said.

Then he looked at Tim's eyes and inside his ears.
"You must have bad ear-ache too, Tim," he said.
Tim nodded.
"You're a brave lad," said Dr Sims.

"Mmm," said Dr Sims. "Up with your jumper, young man."
He put his stethoscope into his ears and listened to
Tim's chest.

"What does that do?" asked Tim.
"I can hear what chests and tummies are saying through it," said Dr Sims. "The sound tells me if people are ill."
Then he let Topsy listen to Tim's heart.

Dr Sims wrote a prescription and gave it to Mummy. "One spoonful four times a day," he said. "This will soon make you feel better, Tim."

Mummy took Topsy and Tim to the Chemist's.
Mrs White, the pharmacist, prepared Tim's
medicine and gave it to Mummy.
"Make sure he takes all the medicine," she said.

Mummy put the medicine safely in her bag.
Just then, Kerry came past.
"I've got some medicine," she said.
"Tim's got some too," said Topsy.

When they got home, Mummy took out the medicine.
It had a special childproof top, but Mummy could
open it. She poured out a spoonful for Tim.
"Did it taste nice?" asked Topsy.
"Mmm," said Tim, licking his lips.

Then Mummy locked the bottle of medicine away
in a cupboard, out of Topsy and Tim's reach.

When Dad came home, Tim was tucking into
blackcurrant jelly. Topsy was not eating hers.
"She's sulking because she isn't ill," said Tim.
"I wonder," said Dad. "Open wide, Topsy,
and let Dr Dad have a look."
Topsy's throat was red and sore.

Dad took Topsy to the Health Centre that evening. Her throat was sore but she was proud to be going to see the doctor.

Dr Sims was not there, so Topsy saw Dr Jaunty instead.
She came home with a bottle of medicine just like Tim's.

*Now turn the page and help
Topsy and Tim solve a puzzle.*

Look at the two pictures.
There are six differences.
Can you spot them all?

A Map of the Village

farm

Topsy and
Tim's house

Tony's
house

Kerr
hou

park

garage

health
centre

post
office

church

primary school

nursery school

police station

Look out for other titles in the series.